P9-DNP-861

POEMS I WROTE WHEN NO ONE WAS LOOKING

ALAN KATZ

with drawings by

EDWARD KOREN

POEMS I WROTE WHEN NO ONE WAS LOOKING

MARGARET K. McELDERRY BOOKS

New York London Toronto Sydney

MARGARET K. McELDERRY BOOKS
An imprint of Simon & Schuster Children's Publishing Division
1230 Avenue of the Americas, New York, New York 10020

Book edited by Emma D. Dryden
Art direction by Polly Kanevsky
The text for this book is set in Futura Standard.
The illustrations for this book are rendered in pen.
Manufactured in the United States of America
0911 FFG
10 9 8 7 6 5 4 3 2 1
Library of Congress Cataloging-in-Publication Data
Katz, Alan.
Poems I wrote when no one was looking / Alan Katz ; drawings by Edward Koren. — 1st ed.
p. cm.
ISBN 978-1-4169-3518-6 (hc)
ISBN 978-1-4424-0274-4 (eBook)
1. Children's poetry, American. 2. Humorous poetry, American.
I. Koren, Edward. II. Title.
PS3561.A745P64 2011
811'.54—dc22
2007052523

To the very poetic Rose;
my love for her just grows and grows.
—A. K.

To my family muses—C+B+N+D+S+J+R
—E. K.

Brushing Up

Grandpa and my
baby sister
are the best of chums.
When they smile,
holy cow, it's
gums, gums, gums, and gums.

Baby sis will get
some teeth
if we just let time pass.
But Grandpa can get his right now;
they're upstairs in a glass.

It Embarrasses Me, a Latte

When Mommy orders coffee,
the clerk there has a laugh.
It's always mocha something,
something, something else,
decaf.
Then skim
blah, blah, blah, blah, blah.
Toppings in odd ratios.
By the time she's finished ordering,
the guy says, "Sorry, closed."

Using My Noodle

I have pasta for every meal.
Plain.
Just plain, plain, plain.
No sauce.
No butter.
No salt.
No spice.
Just pasta,
add water,
and strain.

In My Opinion

Baby sister's hair: shampooable
Mom's library book: renewable
Dad's morning coffee: brewable
Little sister's vitamin: chewable

Me finishing my homework: undoable

That's Entertainment?

Dad's in theater 1
seeing something with fierce action.
Mom's in theater 2
getting crying satisfaction.
Big sis is in 14
shrieking at some vampire guts.
And here I sit alone in 8
watching animated mutts.
I'm glad we didn't stay home
in this very nasty weather.
It's always fun to go out to the movies
all together.

DAD
MOM
SIS

Lend Me Everything But Your Ear . . .

If you lend me a bell,
I will think that you're swell.

If you lend me a movie,
I will think that you're groovy.

If you lend me $12.50,
I will think that you're nifty.

If you lend me your bicycle,
I will think that you're nicycle.

If you lend me your appendix,
I will think you're stupendix.

If you lend me your thesaurus,
I'll find some better rhymes for us.

Numberific

Think of a number
between seven and nine.
Stand back and I'll guess it now:
Eight!
Just how did I know?
Well, I have ESP.
Just call me Amazing Kate!

The Name's the Shame

I know a plumber named Plummer,
a mechanic named Carr,
a lifeguard named Summer,
a golfer named Parr,
a pieman named Baker,
a skier named Hill,
a gardener named Raker,
a tax collector named Bill.

Their jobs are their last names.
To me, that spells doom.
Call if you need sweeping,
'cause I'm Michael Broom.

At the Finished Line

A snail and a
steamroller
had a race.
Well, how 'bout that!
The snail crisscrossed too much
and lost the race
in no time

FLAT!

START

Shortscicle

My brother said he is hot every day
from the second that he gets to school.
I thought quite a lot and I found a good way
to keep my dear brother real cool.

Mom may say that what I am doing is wrong
and I bet she will call me a teaser.
But tonight I made plans
and for this whole night long,
I'll keep his undies in the freezer!

Come for a Spell

I learned to spell Cincinnati,
and it drove me truly batty.
Right at the start, I must confess,
I was confused: a C? An S?
Two Ns then one, or one then two?
I did not know just what to do.
It took a while, and made me cry, oh.
Still, I am fond of Owe–high–yo.

Remote Out-of-Control

Mom yells to me,
"Enough TV!"
I yell back,
"Just till commercial!"

Mom agrees right away
and calls back to me,
"Yes."

I kinda feel bad,
and kinda think Mom
will call my idea controversial.

I'm watching, you see,
all commercial-free
PBS.

Answering the Scrawl

Coloring books are delightful.
Colorful books are such fun.
But baby's in really big trouble, because
the novel Mom's reading
isn't one!

Who, Me?

"I didn't do it!
I didn't do it!"
I told Mom nine times (or ten).
"And if you don't tell Dad tonight,
I promise not to do it again!"

Ch-ch-ch-check, Please

I only eat foods that begin with "c-h,"
Like chicken and churros and chili.
If you're cooking dinner and there's no "c-h,"
then trying to feed me is silly.

Today I had chocolate and chickpeas and chips,
chimichangas and chow mein and cheese.
Tonight, chunky chowder is the only choice—
(Mom is out of "c-h" recipes).

She ordered a cookbook
that's coming tomorrow;
Mom promised great foods she'll be makin'.
It will be a menu of new "c-h" treats—
like chmeatloaf! Chomelets! Chbacon!

No Stopping the Topping

Dad's having a steak;
his plate's covered in red,
which means that he loves ketchup madly.

Or else he just goofed
as he sliced that big steak,
and my poor dad is bleeding quite badly.

Things Are (Not) Looking Up

I just scaled Mount Everest,
then conquered Pike's Peak.
Up and down Kilimanjaro,
in way less than a week.
Climbing is my hobby,
but I am now in a funk.
Because my sister made me take
the scary upper bunk.

DIARY!

This Kid Ain't Kidding Around

My mom is 37.
Her bank code is 5-3-8.
She keeps her extra set of keys
behind the turkey plate.
I'll be glad to read you her diary,
and that is just the beginning.
Next time, I bet she won't make me
leave the game in the third inning!

What Can I Say?

Dad said not to say "butt" anymore.
But he didn't say I couldn't say "but."

Dad said not to say "shut up" anymore.
But he didn't say I couldn't say "shut."

Dad said not to say "nuts" anymore.
But he didn't say I couldn't say "nut."

Dad said not to say "hate your guts" anymore.
But he didn't say I couldn't say "gut."

So, though it doesn't mean anything,
he won't mind my saying "but shut nut gut!"

NO
BUTY
CUTS
SHUT

Commotion Pictures

We went to the three-dollar movies,
so the family could chill and relax.
Twelve bucks for four people to get in.
Not bad.
Then Mom spent ninety-seven on snacks.

Not-So-Special K

If you ask me, we should ban silent K.
"Knife" and "knight"?
Drop the Ks—
my advice.
It does knothing but sit there
and ruin knormal words.
We don't kneed it!
The whole thing's knot knice!

Because You Asked . . .

My sister's name is Cora.
My mother's name is Dora.
My grandpa's Dan.
My grandma's Ann.
My father is a snorer.

My collie's name is Truman.
Around the house he's zoomin'.
He's ninety pounds.
More than most hounds.
(I think he thinks he's human.)

And me? My name is Rosie.
My room is very cozy.
There's more to share,
but I'll stop there.
You really are quite nosy.

Before I Get Old . . .

New Jersey.
New London.
New Hampshire.
New Delhi.
(None of which I've ever been to.)
Someday I'm going to visit 'em all,
stop in and yell out, "Hey,
what's new?"

Rinse-identally . . .

Mom said, "From now on, you do your own wash.
I'm sorry, but that's how it goes."
I can't figure out the washing machine,
so I'm taking a bath in my clothes.

Rattled

I am a baby stuck here in a crib.
People make faces and wave.
Mommy seems nice and she smiles a lot;
Dad's kisses prove he needs a shave.

My sister stops by and goes, "Boo!"
So I cry.
She thinks I'm scared, but I'm not.
I won't forget, and when I'm old enough,
I'll give so much worse than I got.

This whole baby business is really not bad.
They feed me and wipe all my poo.
I'm just a month old.
And uh-oh, here they come.
I gotta stop talking—
Goo goo.

Shhhhh . . .

Please don't bang!
Or slam!
Or buzz!
And please no loud
bansheeing!
Do not click!
And do not clunk!
I'm onomatopoeiaing.

Who's There?

There's a baby in Mommy's tummy.
Boy or girl?
We don't know what it is.
I can't wait to find out,
'cause then I will know
if I'll be a big brother
or sis.

Sick 'Em

I've got a headache.
My throat is sore.
My ears are ringing.
Stomach pain is the worst I've endured.

Hey—look out the window!
There's a whole foot of snow!
No school today!
Guess what?
I'm cured!

101 Donations

If you have prosperity,
it's nice to give to charity.
A cent,
a buck,
a ten,
a mil.
Give what you can,
give what you will.

If those who have
help those who've not,
then those who've not
will have a lot.
And if the ones who *had* then lack,
the ones who *got*
can give some back.

C.L.U.B. Sandwich

I belong to the
N.C.D.S.C.B.D.G.V.,
a division of
the A.M.M.M.S.Y.T.T.
We've never had a meeting.
No other members
have been seen.
And frankly,
I have no idea
what the initials mean.

Good Thing You Got Here Oily

Mom tells me coconut oil
comes from a coconut.
Olive oil is made from olives.
(Could it come from anything but?)
Now Mom has shared some knowledge
and the news just scared me so—
she needs some baby oil.
Oh well, there goes little bro!

Getting to Know Me

My name is Shannon Bannon.
I live at 4 Fleet Street.
I have a pretty kitty
and my dad, Brad, juggles meat.

Okay, you caught me lying.
I do it all the time.

My name is Sue.
I live on Main.
No cat.
I like to rhyme.

I Got Rooked

"Hut, hut, hike!"
"Hut, hut, hike!"
"Hut, hut, hike!"
Brother yells.
His booming voice causes such stress.
I tell him to stop.
Then I tell him again.
After all, we are just playing chess.

A Regular Howldini

Most dogs are good at chasing sticks.
But mine can do great magic tricks.
Like make Dad's slippers disappear.
(His left one's missing for a year!)
And something he can do with ease
is produce a large throng of fleas.
To see him, make a reservation.
His show's called *Prestidogitation*!

Fridge-a-Dare

In my room for weeks
I left some doughnuts good for dunkin'.

By the time Mom found it,
the whole bag was really stunkin'.

Mom said no more food upstairs,
'cept fruit on rare occasions.

I lost a bunch of grapes—
someday they will turn up . . . as raisins.

Nice to See You

We ring when we come to visit.
Gram asks, "Who is it?"

Two hours, and that does it.
Then Grammy asks, "Who was it?"

A Thing of the Past-a

I make believe my spaghetti is worms.
There's a bird outside, and I bet he
does the same thing, just in reverse . . .
he pretends his worms are spaghetti.

Pleasant Dreams, Unpleasant Streams

When I change the baby,
I stand there and I pray
that he lets me do it quickly
and he doesn't start to spray.

My parents named him Francis,
but evidence is mountin';
the more he squirts, the more I'm sure
they should have called him Fountain.

How Inventive!

My name is Albert Feinstein.
I'm here with Thomas Pedison.
We'll meet with Jonas Salkenbaum,
who's working on some medicine.

Well, in flies Benjamin Cranklin!
Henry Fordowitz drove alone.
Alexander Graham Bellman won't be here—
couldn't get him on the phone!

Right Between the Eyes

Dad has a big nose.
Mom has a big nose.
So far, I have quite a small breather.
At this point, I'm okay,
although I gotta say:
Mom's or Dad's nose?
I wouldn't pick either.

Meowch!

Cat on the bathtub.
Cat on the chairs.
Cat on the TV.
Cat on the stairs.
Cat on the window.
Cat on the bed.
Cat on the mantel.
Cat on my head.
Cat on the table.
Cat on the chest.
Cat on the pillow.
Cat is a pest!

The Most Important Story Ever

Fifty-two men,
with ninety-six bags,
and twenty-six goats,
and a duck.
They had quite a mission,
and only an hour.
The townspeople wished them all luck.

The men grabbed the bags
and opened them up.
The goats milled around
and made noise.
The duck led the action
in total command
as a fowl of great vision and poise.

One man yelled, "This
cannot be done, it's too hard!
We need some more bags
and a truck!
Furthermore," the man barked
with a lump in his throat,
"who said, 'You're the boss!' to that duck?"

The goats said, "Hey, yeah!
Who made the duck boss?"
They all fought as time passed,
and how!
Yelling and howling and squawking and mooing.
(A bilingual goat screamed in Cow.)

The man who had started the uproar
then yelled,
"It is time for the fighting to cease!"
They all dropped their bags,
marched past goats and duck,
and stormed away to live in peace.

The duck was confounded.
The goats were confused.
The bags were just speechless.
(Well, duh.)
The men were upset, and they asked,
"Well, what now?"
The outspoken guy shouted,
"Uhhhhhh . . ."

This story is true.
Take my word,
it's all fact.
Though where the men went,
no one knows.
And we never found out
what was inside those bags.
Was it food? Was it toys?
Was it clothes?

Just why they were there
with those goats and that duck?
It's all an historical blur.
Had their mission succeeded,
it could have meant greatness.
Instead, all the world got was
"Uhhhhhh . . ."

The Brush-Off

When Daddy painted the den,
Mom said, "Two coats! Looks great! Happy wife!"
But when I painted
two coats of Mom's,
she got mad—
and I'm grounded for life.

Barking up the Family Tree

I think my sister is a dog.
She usually has fleas.
She chews on Mommy's flip-flops
and she makes our grandma sneeze.
She likes her belly tickled
and she chases a toy mouse.
I am surprised our parents let her live
inside the house.

This Just In . . .

My brother was stealing.
Dad shot him.
We watched.

Please don't be upset,
and don't chafe.
Dad shot with a camera.
Bro was stealing third.
So relax.
By the way,
he was safe!

Lesson the Damage

If you're playing bullfighter,
don't be the bull at all.
And if you do,
make sure that you
don't charge where there's a wall.

If you're playing parachute,
here's something you should hear:
Never, ever, ever
jump down from the chandelier.

If you're playing stunt driver,
do not race at warp speed.
In fact, I'd recommend
you just stay in the house
and read!

Come What May

March! March! March!
March! March! March!
March! March! March!
I will.
It's the only way
I can remember
the month before April!

Where, Oh Where, Oh Where?

Mom misplaced her car keys,
also her phone book.
Mom misplaced her iPod.
Through the house, we've helped her look.

Mom said she would pay us,
but I know that won't be true.
Because when she misplaced those things,
she lost her wallet, too!

The Bad Cold

Mike gave it to Danny,
who then passed it on to Manny,
who then shared it with Marissa,
also Roger and Alissa.
Alissa coughed near Bobby,
and 'cause Bobby's really slobby,
he infected Al and Clara, Rick and
Sue, Annette and Lara.
Then somehow it got to Prudence.
So Ms. Smith has got no students.

COVER YOUR MOUTH WHEN YOU COUGH
DON'T SNEEZE IN ANYONE'S FACE
DON'T TOUCH ANYONE
DON'T LEAVE USED TISSUES LYING AROUND

The Fizz Biz

If someone shakes a soda can,
and says that they will share it,
don't be the one
who pops the top . . .
or you will surely wear it!

Vegging Out

I don't have a father.
I don't have a mother.
I don't have a sister.
I don't have a brother.
But please do not feel sorry
and don't you get all sad-ish.
I do not need a family.
After all, I am a radish.

Checkup (and Down)

The dentist advised,
"Up and down, fifty times."

When I tried, Mom said I aggravate her.

Though I cried, "He was clear—
up and down, fifty times!"
She yelled, "Get out of that elevator!"

I Feel Alphabetter Already

I take Vitamin A,
Vitamin B,
Vitamin C,
and Vitamin D.
If the body can't use 'em,
it'll refuse 'em.
And then what will
I see?
Vitamin P(ee).

Maybe I Should Try Glassical?

Listening to rock
isn't usually bad.
But, boy, did Mommy complain
when the rock
that she heard
was the one that I tossed
right through our living room
windowpane.

That's Showbiz

When I grow up,
I'm gonna be
a movie star and on TV.

I now would be glad to act for you,
but sorry, I'm strictly
Pay-Per-View.

Handy Candy

"Don't take too many gumdrops!"
Mom yells from down the hall.
How many is too many?
Don't know,
and so,
I think I'll take 'em all.

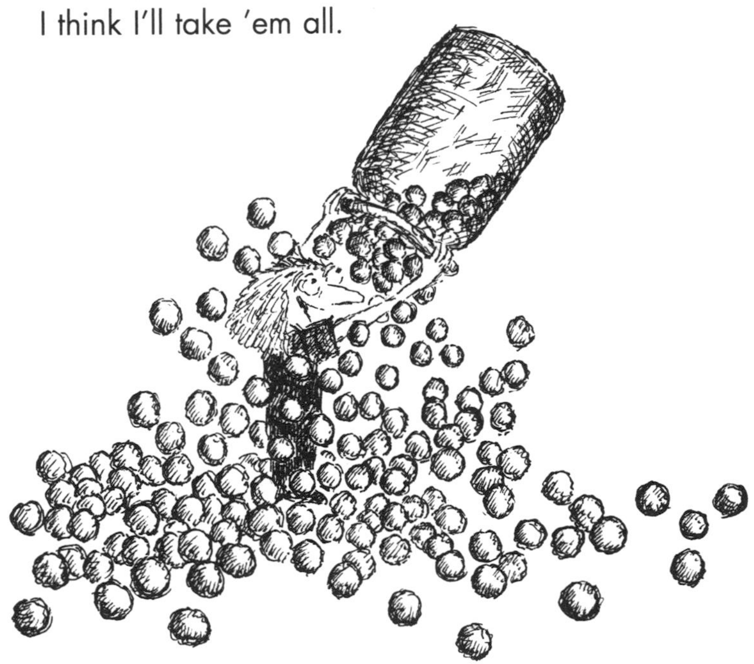

May I Haf Your Addemtion?

We need a new P.A. system
throughout our entire school.
'Cause we just heard the principal tell us,
"Goog morging, and felgum to smool."

He wished "Lifa" a "big hassy mirshday,"
then asked all to please "saluk the frag."
I would call the principal and ask him to fix it,
but it might make him amgry or mag.

SCREECH

Am I Being Shellfish?

I think Mom thinks we're crustaceans,
because I heard her blab:
"Our neighbor is a worthless shrimp,
and Daddy is a crab."
Talk like that can make a mess
and get Mom in some tussles.
Although she's right in one small way—
I do have real big mussels.

My Workweak

I have a report due Friday.
It's Monday.
Let's watch a show!

I have a report due Friday.
It's Tuesday.
Big game? Let's go!

I have a report due Friday.
It's Wednesday.
Still time, although . . .

I have a report due Friday.
It's Thursday.
Please, please, PLEASE . . . snow!

I Heard This from Denise Reiss

Two geese in Greece,
one aunt, one niece.
They flew and they
disturbed the peace.

They robbed a man,
and he yelled, "Cease!
You geese give me back my
hairpiece!"

They didn't cease,
those geese in Greece.
So the man shouted,
"Help! Police!"

"Crime will decrease,"
said the police.
(Whose names happened to be
Maurice.)
"If bald men each get
a valise
and hide their hair from
geese who fleece."

The man said to his wife,
Clarisse,
"Perhaps we ought to move to
Nice."

And so they did.
They took a lease.
And saw their happiness
increase.

Until one day, that man
in France
had a reindeer steal
his pants.

Deer Me!

A buck had some dough,
and a doe had some bucks,
so they went on a shopping spree large.
But the stampeding bison
was broke,
so to shop
he had no other choice but to charge.

Stool Pigeon

I'm about to get my brother in trouble,
though he didn't do anything wrong.
He's been a perfect angel every day,
this whole well-behaved week long.

Still, I really could use some excitement,
so I think I'll tell Mom he was bad.
I could say he used really foul language,
which then Mom would go share with Dad.

Then my brother would surely get punished—
no TV, no playdates, no bike.
Mom would see that he's bad and that I'm really good.
(Even though we are so much alike.)

Big Change

My sister stopped wearing diapers,
so I gave her a hug.
I'm really pretty proud, though
it's a good thing
her room has a brown rug.

The Better Letter

My favorite letter of the alphabet
is very plain to see.
It is the fourth,
and can you guess?
It's good old letter D.
Yes, D starts everything I like:
doughnuts and dogs and dance;
diamonds (like for baseball);
darts and dungarees (that's pants).

Though D also starts "dentist" (ouch!);
on a test, it's a bad grade.
And D is right up front in "dark,"
of which I am afraid.
So D is pretty good, I guess.
It's not such a bad letter.
But C is cake and candy.
So now,
that's my favorite letter.

Punctured Punctuation

I don't like the ampersand.
You can't hold it in your h&.
I'm not crazy 'bout the comma.
It adds pauses, too much drama.
I don't like parentheses.
(Keep them away from me, please.)
I also hate the asterisk.
Though I do like to eat hot bisque.*

*A thick, creamy soup often made from lobster.

The United Scrapes of America

I went to Maine
and bumped my brain.

Then in Fort Drum
I jammed my thumb.

Next went to Meade
where I got kneed.

In Idaho
I broke my toe.

Good old Duluth?
Good guess—a tooth.

I do get hurt each place I go.
But in Oregon, alas.
I'm not gonna take any chances,
and I'll totally skip
Grants Pass.

MY DIARY
Zale

Good Buy, Good Buy, Good Buy!

Garage sale! Garage sale!
All this stuff must go!

I've realized that if you take
Mom and Daddy's things to sell 'em,
it's a really, really good idea
before you do, to tell 'em.

Sister's slippers, fifty cents!
Gotta raise some dough
to buy back all the things I sold
at my sale a week ago!

It's Tutu Much!

Grandma dragged me to the ballet
for the first time.
And if you ask, I will say
'twas the worst time.
Prancing around in their undies—
absurd!

And we sat so far away,
I couldn't hear
a word!

Route, Route, Route for the Home Team

My father has a GPS.
It gives us great directions.
It tells us which highway to take.
It finds us intersections.
It helps us get most anywhere,
no matter near or far.
In fact, it got us to this mall—
but now we can't find our car.

Brotherly Love?

The lint in my brother's navel—
blah!
It's so furry in there.
He's saving it, he says,
for me
to stuff a teddy bear.

The wax in my brother's ears—
big yuck!
It's more than I can handle.
He's saving it, he says,
and soon
he's gonna have a candle.

The Winner Takes It All

I won a million tickets
while at the town arcade.
I threw the ball!
I bopped the moles!
I chased the light brigade!

I want a horse!
A stereo!
A boat, perhaps a jet!
A million tickets!
Who knows what
a kid like me can get!

I can't wait to redeem them
and now, the time has come.
Look, for my million tickets,
I get . . .
a piece of gum!

What I Wish

I wish for peace.
I wish that war right now would cease.
I wish that poverty were a thing of the past,
and harmony among people would always last.
I wish that hungry people had stomachs full.
But if I wish too much,
I'll just take a bicycle.

Just Curious

A pair is always two,
like sock plus sock
or shoe plus shoe.
Which is why I ask—
answer if you dare:
Why's there just one
in a pair of
underwear?

Holy Cow Juice!

My brother is so wacky.
My brother is so weird.
I've seen kids get milk mustaches,
but he's got a milk beard!

Zzzz . . .

I've been sitting and waiting,
and waiting,
and waiting
for an hour,
or two,
or more.
I've been waiting,
and I've no idea
just what I'm waiting for.

It's Better to Give . . .

Tomorrow's Mommy's birthday
and I don't have a gift.
I want to give her something
that will give her a big lift.
I could get her some jewelry—
that would certainly bring cheer.
It's better than the headache
she said I gave her last year.

HAPPY
MOM
BIRTHDAY

Roll On!

Mommy walks real slowly;
she is wearing giant heels.
I can go much faster,
'cause I've got built-in wheels.
But when we're in a hurry,
we ditch those heels and wheels.
And *zoom zoom zoom*, we're on our way
thanks to automobiles.

Stop Needling Me!

"Please draw some blood,"
Doc says.
I cried.
I like my blood to stay
inside.

The nurse says,
"I'll give you this sticker."
Should I take it?
Should I kick her?

"I'll throw in a paddle game."
That's cool . . . but I squirm just the same.
I writhe! I turn! Flail left and right.
That's when she offers a flashlight.

Each time I jerk, another thing
she offers. It gets interesting.
Then my best move—I do the thrash.
And then she says, "How 'bout some cash?"

She got the blood
(and she took plenty).
By the way,
got change of twenty?

What a Gas!

My two brothers,
Mom and Dad, and I
went to the Museum of Fine Arts.
We had spicy food right before we arrived—
now it's the Museum of Five Farts.

The Matter Is Clothed

You ask if I'm dressed
and ready to go.
Well, Mom,
I'd have to say sorta.
I put on my socks
and also my shoes.
But not, I'm afraid,
in that order.

Mom and Pop(corn)

I'm with Mom and Dad at the movies.
They're holding hands;
Dad starts to mutter.
His hand keeps slipping off of hers—
guess I got too much butter.

All I Need

I've got a DVD,
a handheld game,
some markers,
and some crackers.
A bag of popcorn, also chips.
(My folks are real good packers.)
When you have lots of stuff to do
and eat, the backseat rocks.

I'm set for this whole trip, though
we're just going seven blocks.

Zzzz . . .
(Part Two)

I just found out—
amazing news!
Seems you were my appointment.
I waited,
and waited
so long for you . . .
what a huge disappointment!

Uh-Oh!

There is no poem on this page—
the publisher made a mistake.
Which really is too bad,
because I wrote one
called "The Lake."
It really was quite beautiful.
The editor said she cried.
It touched her and it made her feel
all warm down deep inside.
The swans! The fish! The picnickers!
The birds! The red canoe!
It's a shame you'll never see it,
'cause you would have loved it too.
It would have been an epic, and
award groups I could thank.
But none of that will happen,
because this whole page is blank.

Weather or Not

Snap snap snap snap snap snap.
Clip clip clip clip clip.
Flap flap flap flap flap flap.
Zip zip zip zip zip.
Clomp clomp clomp clomp clomp clomp.
Mitts mitts mitts mitts mitts.
I can't move in this snowsuit—
next year, please get me one that fits.

Smooch

Eskimos kiss with their noses.
Americans kiss with their lips.
I wish that my cousin would never kiss me,
'cause she's two and her nose always drips.

Eater's Digest

"Hot bread! Fresh butter!
Cold water!" we yell.
The service seems slow and contrary.

A man finally visits our table and says,
"No food here—
you're in a library!"

ROS-
TAB

The Bucks Stop Here

Daddy can be very forgetful,
Dad's memory is so bad.
Our family just had a big meal
in a diner,
and Father just did something sad.
He put ten bucks down on the table,
then left the place just like a rocket.

But never fear, his loving son's on the job—
I grabbed the cash and stuffed it in my pocket!

Crust Bust

When the pizza man threw up his pizza,
it twirled and we all aahed and oohed.
But when I had too much,
and I threw up my slice—
my mom and dad said I was rude.

Wish You Were Here Here

Walla Walla.
Bora Bora.
New York, New York.
All nice.
I've been to each place once.
To tell you,
gotta say them twice.

A Real Meal Deal

My very cheap grandfather
took me to an
Italian restaurant.
Although he's cheap
(I told you that),
he said, "Get what you want."
I had a lot of entrées,
though I did lose count how many.
And Grandpa got real mad
'cause he was counting every penne.

Feeding Time

The time is now 2:52.
Time to feed the kangaroo.
The time is now 2:53.
Time to feed the chimpanzee.
The time is now 2:54.
Time to feed the dinosaur.
The time is now 2:55.
Time to feed the whole beehive.
The time is now 2:56.
Time to feed the baby chicks.
The time is now 2:57.
Time for me to eat (I'm Kevin).

Disconcerting

My sister plays the violin—
we're here at her recital.
To compliment her at the end,
Mom says is really vital.
She screeches and she scratches,
and I know she's really trying.
Not sure if this is *Clair de Lune*,
or outside, a cat's dying.

Mattress Stress

It's 7 a.m.
I have a headache.
It's thumping
and pounding.
The worst!
From now on, I'll know,
and I'll never forget:
Always get out of bed by feet first!

Look What I Invented!

I left my books on the library lawn.
While home that night, I missed 'em.
I ran right back the following morn
and began the dewy decimal system.

Finger Food

My sister threw out her knife and fork
when she dumped her plate of pork.
Mom didn't get mad.
Well, what could she say?
Sis never uses 'em anyway.

Please Don't Feed the People

The zoo is quite a lively place,
such creatures—
all so rude!
Look at how that big one eats,
no manners, my, how crude!
And how that small one yelps when mad;
it's loud beyond its age!

And that is why I'm really glad
to watch them from my cage!

It Doesn't Compute

Daddy's downloading music.
Mommy's downloading pix.
Sister's downloading homework.
Brother's downloading flicks.
Grandma's downloading health forms,
and I have a really big hunch:
They're so busy on their computers,
no one's free to download me lunch.

I Got a Bad Coif

Mom's hair is straight.
Mom's hair is red.
Mom's hair is blond and curly.
She changes it so often,
she must get up really early.

It was just spiked.
But now it's waved
all in the same direction.
It could be Mom's the owner of
a giant wig collection.

The way she switches hairdos,
there's no way to analyze her.
It's mostly cool, though there are times
we do not recognize her.

With Dad, it's simpler of course,
his hair changes are tiny.
There's been no style in a while—
'cause his dome's smooth and shiny.

Poem 100

This is it, poem one hundred!
Hope you had a lot of fundred!
In the rain, or in the sundred . . .
if you liked this book,
I'll write another onedred.

'Bye!

Oh, wait,
I can't end this book like that.
Here's some friendly advice,
from me to you,
in poetic form.
I hope you follow it daily.
Or weekly.
Or monthly.
Or never.

Keep smiling.
Keep reading.
Keep dialing.
Keep weeding.
Keep writing.
Keep waving.
Keep biting.
Keep shaving.
Keep hoping.
Keep dreaming.
Keep soaping.
Keep beaming.
Keep breathing.
Keep giving.
Keep teething.
Keep living.

Index of Titles

Index of First Lines